THIS WALKER BOOK BELONGS TO:

_____

_____

_____

_____

For Anna-Katerina

First published 2000 by Walker Books Ltd
87 Vauxhall Walk, London SE11 5HJ

This edition published 2001

2 4 6 8 10 9 7 5 3 1

© 2000 Julie Lacome

This book has been typeset in Humana Sans

Printed in Hong Kong

British Library Cataloguing in Publication Data:
a catalogue record for this book is
available from the British Library

ISBN 0-7445-7877-9

RuTHiE's BiG OLD CoAT

JuLiE LACOME

WALKER BOOKS
AND SUBSIDIARIES
LONDON • BOSTON • SYDNEY

The coat used to belong
to Ruthie's cousin Frances.
Now it was Ruthie's turn
to wear it.

"This big old coat is too big,"
said Ruthie.
"You'll grow into it,"
said Mummy.

Ruthie tried to grow. Nothing happened.

Ruthie marched outside. "This big old coat is too big," she said. Her friend Fiona from next door giggled.

"It *is* big," said Fiona. "It's big enough for me, too!"
She scooted inside and did up the zip.

Ruthie and Fiona
did the tango,
the twist,
and the
four-legged
turkey trot.

They played Monster,

Big Red
Air Balloon,

and DANGER Poisonous Mushroom.

They zoomed across the garden on Fiona's skateboard.

Ruthie looked at Fiona
in the big old coat.

Fiona looked at Ruthie
in the big old coat.

They got a big case of the Big Old Coat Giggles.

All of a sudden, Ruthie stopped laughing.
All of a sudden, Ruthie needed to
go to the toilet.

Fiona tugged and tugged, but the zip
was stuck!

"The zip won't unstick, it won't, it won't,"
cried Fiona.

"Forget the zip," said Ruthie. "I've got to go NOW!"

"Zoinks!" yelled Fiona. "Let's run for it!"

Fiona said she wouldn't
look and Ruthie scrunched
her trousers down and …

Ahh!

"Oh Ruthie," Mummy said
   as she unstuck the zip.
"This coat really is
   too big and too old."

"Oh Mummy," said Ruthie, giving her
  a kiss, "we love this coat."
"Zoinks!" said Fiona. "It's perfect!"

The coat *was* perfect.
It was perfect for
Twin-engine Aeroplane
Gone Loco …

and perfect for the biggest-ever case
of the Big Old Coat Giggles.

JULIE LACOME based **Ruthie's Big Old Coat** on a true story involving herself, a big *new* coat and a friend called Fiona. She says, "My mum bought me the coat when I was little, and it had plenty of room for growth. My friend Fiona decided that it was big enough for both of us and climbed inside with me and zipped it up. We played and giggled for a while until Fiona needed to go to the toilet. But the zip was stuck. Unlike the characters in the book, unfortunately we didn't reach the toilet in time ... and there was a puddle!"

Julie Lacome hails from a very artistic family and so it is not surprising that her interest in art was encouraged from an early age. She has worked as a freelance illustrator for magazines, greetings card manufacturers and the BBC, where she illustrated pictures for use on *Playschool*. She is well known for her colourful collage illustrations, which have immense appeal for the very young. Already to her credit on the Walker list are *Walking Through the Jungle*; *I'm a Jolly Farmer*; *The Shape of Things* and *Sing a Song of Sixpence*. Julie lives in Edinburgh.

ISBN 0-7445-3643-X (pb)

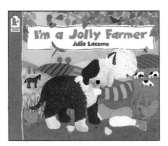

ISBN 0-7445-4382-7 (pb)

ISBN 0-7445-4368-1 (pb)

ISBN 0-7445-5427-6 (pb)